O'Brien Press Memo
From: The Management
To: All Members of Staff
Subject: The Forbidden Files

You're probably wondering why you arrived this
morning to find the police searching your desks.

The safe containing the Forbidden Files was broken
into. The Files have been STOLEN.

The stories in these Files were kept locked up and
hidden away for good reason.
These stories are too
FRIGHTENING, too DISTURBING or
just too downright DISGUSTING
to be read by children.

The police will want to speak
to all of you — please give
them your full cooperation.
We have to find The Forbidden
Files; they must NEVER see the
light of day.

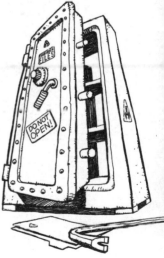

TOO
LATE,
SUCKERS!

Have You Seen This Man?

OISÍN McGANN grew up in the suburban backstreets of Dublin and Drogheda. He has never had a **proper job**, but he has written and illustrated numerous children's books of **questionable quality**. McGann is known as a **loner** with few friends. If you should see this man, **do not approach him,** as he may be **rude**.

WIRED TEETH

Written & Illustrated by

Oisín McGann

THE O'BRIEN PRESS
DUBLIN

First published 2008 by The O'Brien Press Ltd,
12 Terenure Road East, Rathgar, Dublin 6, Ireland
Tel: +353 1 4923333; Fax: +353 1 4922777
E-mail: books@obrien.ie
Website: www.obrien.ie

ISBN: 978-1-84717-003-3

British Library Cataloguing-in-Publication Data
McGann, Oisin
Wired teeth. - (Forbidden files)
1. Children's stories
I. Title
823.9'2[J]

1 2 3 4 5 6 7 8 9
08 09 10 11

The O'Brien Press
receives assistance from

the arts
council
an chomhairle
ealaíon

Layout and design: The O'Brien Press
Printed and bound in the UK by CPI Bookmarque, Croydon

CONTENTS

1

Terror In The Classroom

Jason McGinty was a bad kid, but his teeth were worse. At this moment, they were leering wickedly at an unfortunate fourth class pupil who had the bad luck to catch Jason's eye as he came out into the playground at break-time.

'What you lookin' at?' Jason snarled, baring his horribly jagged, crooked teeth.

'Nothing!' the ten-year-old cowered. 'I wasn't looking at anything!'

'You're lookin' at me now. And you're talkin' to me. Did I say you could talk to me?' Jason persisted.

The younger kid's mouth shut with a stifled squeak.

'Answer me!' Jason shouted.

His victim went pale as he struggled to work out which was more likely to get him beaten up – talking, or not talking. He couldn't tell. Maybe both.

Jason gave the younger boy another close look at his teeth, and then shoved him backwards for good measure, sending him stumbling onto his backside.

'Watch yourself in future,' he snapped. 'You're on my list now, right?'

With that, he walked off to where his posse of mates were looking on in amusement.

'You're in a bit of a mood, Jayo,' Vince said to him. 'What's got up your nose?'

'Your bad breath, ye smelly git,' Jason retorted, and they all cackled noisily.

That was his favourite sound, his mates laughing. And he made them laugh more than anyone else. He was The Man. Nobody messed with Jason McGinty. But Vince was right; Jason was in a bit of a mood. In fact, that morning, Jason was being extra-aggressive because he was scared – scared like a little kid being chased by a big dog. He was getting a half day today. Normally that would be a good thing – a great thing – but not today.

Because today he was going to see his orthodontist, a kind of dentist who straightened teeth.

This was his third orthodontist, to be exact. The first one had taken one look at Jason's teeth and had a nervous breakdown right there on the spot. The second one had nearly lost two fingers when Jason accidentally bit down during an examination. The man's sleeve had tickled his nose, making him sneeze, his fearsome array of teeth snapping closed like a bear-trap. Jason's mother had rushed the unfortunate man to the hospital, but he had made it clear he never wanted to see Jason or his teeth again.

This third fellow, though, was different. He got giddy when he first saw Jason's teeth. The X-rays that showed those impossibly contorted molars, the twisted canines, the zig-zag incisors, they brought an excited grin to the face of this orthodontist. And that worried Jason. Nobody else smiled when they looked at his teeth.

When the bell rang at the end of break, all the children filed reluctantly back to their classrooms. Jason found his favourite victim, Fintan, already sitting at his desk like the swot he was. Miss Taylor wasn't back from the staffroom yet, so Jason seized the opportunity to grab Fintan's pencil case, unzip it, and hurl its contents across the room. The large collection of pens, set squares and carefully sharpened pencils scattered everywhere. His posse laughed heartily as they took their seats, watching Fintan scamper around on the floor between the desks, trying to pick up his stuff. He was pushed and hustled as the other kids hurried to their desks. He kept his head down, trying not to show the hurt on

his face. This was just another bit of hassle in a whole life full of hassle.

'Get your act together, Fintan,' Vince called. 'Honestly, you're so clumsy.'

'You'll need this, Fintan,' Jason waved the *Fireflight* pencil case.

Fintan straightened up, and went to grab it, but he was too slow. Jason tossed it to Tony, on the other side of the room. Tony waited for Fintan to come after it, but Fintan knew better by now. He humbly took his seat, and laid the handful of pencils and pens out loose on his desk. His face was full and red, like it was going to burst, and he was careful not to look at anybody else. The posse knew he wouldn't squeal on them. That was the beauty of it; he could seek the protection of the teacher, but the teacher couldn't be there all the time, and once she was out of sight, the lads would make it twice as bad for getting them in trouble. They'd really get nasty then. And squealing would lose him whatever respect he had left in the yard. So Fintan just shut up and took it, like the good boy he was. Some of the other kids were laughing, mainly the posse. The rest just ignored him.

'You're a funny man, Jason McGinty,' Sonia Singh said.

'Getting funnier every day,' her twin sister, Anita, added.

Jason turned to look at them. They were smiling, but not with proper smiles. They had this look on their faces like they knew something he didn't. They were always giving him that look. He never knew if

they were taking the mickey out of him or not, and that really annoyed him.

He shot an exaggerated frown at them, and they both crossed their eyes at him at exactly the same time. It was spooky how they could do that. He opened his mouth to make a smart remark, but Miss Taylor walked in just then, and he shut it again.

The class was boring. Boring maths and then history until lunch. Jason sat through both lessons with his jaws clenched shut, unable to stop thinking about what was coming. Normally, when the lunch bell rang, he was the first one out of his seat. This time it seemed to ring deep and slow, like a funeral bell. He started to slowly put his things into his bag.

The school secretary leaned in the door as the other children flooded out like a herd of miniature wildebeest.

'Jason? Your mother's here.'

2

The Remote Control Contraption

Jason sat trembling with tension in Dr Shapiro's waiting room.

'There's nothing to worry about, Jason,' his mother said. 'Children get braces put on every day of the week. And ... and he's supposed to be very good. That little girl from round the corner had her braces put on here, and look at her teeth now!'

Jason sniffed. That little girl from round the corner used to have buck teeth. He'd have given his right arm just to have buck teeth. She used to look like a rabbit; he looked like a shark that had been chewing on an iron bar. It wasn't the same thing.

'You'll be fine,' his mother reassured him.

But she sounded almost as scared as he was. He thought about his hero, John Crater, from the *Fireflight* films. He wouldn't have been scared of an orthodontist. Jason glanced uneasily towards the surgery door. The only thing was, John Crater had perfect teeth.

The nurse came in, a clipboard in her hand, dressed in a clean white uniform.

'Jason McGinty,' she said, and a shiver ran down Jason's spine.

He tried to act brave, he really did. But as he was led away from his mother, walking through to the hallway and into the surgery, his breath was catching like he was going to cry, and his legs were trembling. He had been in the surgery once before, but that was just so Dr Shapiro could have a look at him, and make a mould of his teeth. That had been bad enough, the big lump of putty – or whatever it was – filling his mouth had made him feel like he was choking. This time the weird tooth-fanatic was going to *operate*.

'Ah, young Mr McGinty,' the orthodontist welcomed him with an eager smile. 'Hop up on that seat there, and let's get you sorted out.'

He was a pale, scrawny man, with tufts of sandy-coloured hair, and the smallest hands Jason had ever seen on an adult. His eyes were always open a little too wide. Jason took a deep breath, and did as he was told.

The seat was cool. Jason wished he had one at home for sitting in while he was playing his games. The rest of the room gave him the creeps. It was mostly like a dentist's surgery – with the tools and lamps and the mask for the laughing gas – which

made him uncomfortable as it was. But there were some bizarre-looking machines sitting around on the counters too, stuff he hadn't even seen in the

other orthodontist's surgeries. Stuff that looked like
Shapiro had invented it himself. Jason's teeth were
chattering as he lay back in the chair.

'That's it,' the man said gently, leaning over him and switching on the big angle-poise lamp. 'Now, open wide.'

Jason did as he was told. Dr Shapiro managed to get both of his miniature hands into Jason's mouth as he poked and prodded around. Jason could tell he was really excited.

'Good, good,' he said to himself.

Jason wondered what was so good about it.

'Right, well I think it's time to get started,' the orthodontist said, standing up straight again, and picking up some tools. Hard, sharp, thin, steel tools.

'As you know, you have a rather ... a rather unusual dental profile, and I just don't think the standard "train-tracks" would do the job. A little bit too ... *conventional*. I think this calls for something special – a little contraption I've come up with myself. I love that word, "contraption", don't you?'

No, Jason didn't like it. It made him want to wet himself with terror.

'This won't hurt too much,' Shapiro said softly.

'Here. Bite down on this.'

He stuck something in Jason's mouth, and when Jason bit down, there was a snapping noise. Jason yelped as he felt something grip his teeth.

'No need to worry,' Shapiro assured him. 'That's

just the frame. Here we go now.'

And then he began his work. He explained every-thing as he did it, and despite the abject fear of the ordeal, Jason found the man's voice comforting. And when Shapiro wasn't talking, he hummed to himself, interrupted every now and again by a grunt while he had to twist or tighten something.

First, he attached an anchor point to each tooth, carefully cementing each into place in much the same way that Jason put together his model aeroplanes. Then he wound sturdy pieces of wire through them, tightening them like guitar strings, testing them, adjusting them, taking them out and putting them back in again. When he had them properly 'tuned', he used a screwdriver to turn something along the inside of Jason's cheek, and the wires suddenly constricted all around his teeth at once. By now, Jason was nearly in tears, and he could feel the tension spread from his jaw up into his head.

'It will feel a bit tight to begin with, but you'll get

used to it,' Dr Shapiro said. 'And you won't have to wear those silly straps around your head at night like with some braces. No, these are state-of-the art! You see, these are *smart* braces.'

He opened up a laptop computer and showed Jason the screen.

'A microprocessor in the braces reads how much tension is needed from one minute to the next, and sends the information to this computer. Here are your teeth on the screen, see?'

Jason nodded, fascinated despite the pain. He could see a computer image of his teeth on the screen, with the braces around them. It was like looking at a ghostly, green skull.

'The computer takes that information,' Shapiro went on, 'and sends commands to the braces when they're too loose or causing you too much pain, et cetera et cetera ... So they work with *maximum efficiency.*'

'So my braces are on remote control?' Jason asked, wincing as the words made his jaw ache.

'Precisely,' Shapiro smiled. 'It's amazing what we can do with computers these days.'

*   *   *

When they got home, Jason's mother let him watch two *Fireflight* films on DVD, to help him forget the discomfort of the braces. It still took him a long time to get to sleep that night. His jaw hurt, and he spent a long time looking in the

mirror before going to bed. Half of him hated what he saw, the other half relished the thought of going into school looking like a monster, like one of the villains from *Fireflight*. But he remembered all the kids he'd slagged for having train-track braces, and knew they'd be laughing at him tomorrow.

Jason lay awake, thinking about what he would have to do to stop them laughing.

3

Making An Example
Of Fintan

His mother always dropped him off to school early, on her way to work. This was fine with Jason, because that was normally when he crammed his homework in, trading answers with his mates in the half hour before the bell rang. He didn't have any homework to do this morning; but as he walked into school with his lips tightly closed, his brain was working overtime. There was a strange tingling in his teeth, which for some reason reminded him of static on a radio.

He was surprised to find he was nervous about going into the yard. Usually, *he* was the reason *other* people were nervous. On an empty lot opposite the school was a huge, steel phone mast that had gone up earlier in the year. Standing in its shadow, reluctant to cross the road to school, Jason remembered when the towering mast had been built.

All the parents had protested against it, because they said it would mess with their children's brains. The children, on the other hand, had been delighted. They thought school was already messing with their heads, and this way they'd at least get a better signal on their mobile phones.

That was until the thing was finished, and all the kids found out the signal on their phones was *worse* than before. They had joined their parents in their protest, and had made banners and everything. That had been fun, they'd missed nearly a week of school over it. But now the tower meant he couldn't call his mum and tell her he was feeling sick, and wanted to go home. Not without going into the school. He would just have to 'bite the bullet', like John Crater always said.

His class normally gathered in the same place in the yard, near the door to their room, and some of them were already there. He found Fintan sitting against the wall with a book open on his lap. The sap was always reading. Jason went up to him and leaned his face in close.

'Hey, Fintan,' he said, loud enough for everyone to hear him. 'What do ya think of my new braces?'

Fintan looked up as Jason bared his teeth at him. Jason saw the corners of his mouth begin to curl into a smile, and savagely grabbed him by his ears, pulling him onto his feet.

'What did you say?' he snarled.

'I didn't say anything!' Fintan protested.

'You made a crack about my braces, y'little git. Say it again, or don't you have the guts to say it to my face?'

'I didn't say a thing!' Fintan whined, frantically.

Jason saw more of his class walking up towards them, and knew this was the time. He swung his knee hard into Fintan's thigh, giving him a dead leg. Fintan collapsed to the ground, crying. Jason took out his carton of milk, opened it, and splashed some over his unwitting victim's hair. Fintan would wipe the worst of it off, but in the summer heat, it would be smelling before the end of the day.

Jason stood over him, his fist held out.

'Don't you EVER try it on with me, or I'll kill ya, you little prat! D'you hear me?'

But it didn't matter if Fintan heard him. Fintan had learned that lesson long ago. It was the rest of the class, everyone else, who had to hear him.

As he walked away, Jason heard a voice from somewhere close by, but tinny, like it was on a radio:

'*Orange to Indigo. We have the last element. The Tormentor is good to go.*'

4

Mixed Signals

Making an example of Fintan worked; nobody said a thing about his braces until break-time, when the five lads who made up his posse gathered around to check out Dr Shapiro's handywork.

'They look serious,' Vince whistled. 'Do they hurt?'

'Not much,' Jason said casually.

'Do they catch on the insides of your cheeks?' Tony asked.

He had train-tracks, and sometimes they cut the inside of his mouth.

'No,' Jason replied. 'I mean, they feel really big in

my mouth, but they're not sticking out anywhere, y'know? The guy said they were, like, future technology kind of thing.'

He explained how they worked by remote control. The lads were suitably impressed.

'Cool,' said Vince.

There was a crackling sound, and then:

'*Orange, this is Indigo; Subject Alpha is engaging in social interaction with his associates. Situation normal.*'

'What?' Jason grunted.

'What?' Vince asked.

'Who said that about engaging in social whatyamacallit?' Jason retorted.

'What you talkin' about?'

'*Roger that, Indigo. Orange out.*'

Jason flinched, and then looked at the questioning faces of his posse.

'You didn't hear that?'

'Hear what?' Tony asked, a sly smile forming on his face.

Jason knew that smile, and the sideways glance

towards the others. He knew it because he did it often enough himself. Tony was getting ready to slag him.

'You don't hear that?' Jason pressed him. He put his hand to his ear, and then held his palm out to Tony. 'Here, listen.'

On reflex, Tony turned his ear towards the hand to listen, and Jason slapped him lightly on the face.

'That's the sound of you lookin' like an eejit!'

The other boys laughed, and Jason cackled with

them, but his eyes were casting fearfully around.

'*Subjects are laughing at a practical joke.*'

'I have to go to the jacks,' Jason spluttered. 'Back in a sec.'

He sauntered away, trying not to look bothered. But there was no mistaking that voice he had heard. Why hadn't the other lads heard it too? He needed a bit of time on his own, to think. As he strode through the door, the Singh Twins were coming out. Jason gave them a surreptitious glance, and brushed past them.

'Was that a surreptitious glance, you just gave us, Jayo?' Anita asked.

'And he brushed past us too,' Sonia added. 'You're supposed to hold the door open for girls. Didn't you know that?'

They both gave him the same smug smile at exactly the same time.

Too distracted to come up with anything smart to say, he slammed the door on them, and made a face, pressing his nose against the window.

'Mind you don't crack the glass,' Anita chirped, and then they skipped away together.

Those Singh Twins. He couldn't figure them out.

Barging into the boy's toilets, he hurried into one of the cubicles, bolted the door, and sat down on the loo seat. Something weird was going on, and he didn't know what. He let out an exasperated sigh. With nobody around, he felt safe; he stuck his finger up his nose, rooted around for a good lump and then licked the snot off his fingertip.

'Orange, this is Mauve. Subject Alpha has moved to the boy's toilets. He is currently picking his nose.'

Jason stood up with a jolt, staring around at the walls of the cubicle, up at the ceiling, and down at the gap under the door.

'*Roger that, Mauve. Keep me posted. Orange out.*'

'Who's there?!' he shrieked. 'I'll ... I'll rip your flippin' heads off if you're messin' with me! What do you want?'

'I just want to go to the toilet,' a small child's fearful voice squeaked from the next cubicle. 'But I can't while you're shoutin' at me.'

His cheeks hot and flushed with embarrassment, Jason threw the door open and rushed back to his classroom.

5

The Face In The Window

It wasn't like him to stay in at break, and the teachers always made the children go outside when the weather was all right. He found Fintan sitting at his desk near the window, writing something in a copybook. All worked up like he was, Jason wanted to be on his own, but at least he wouldn't get any hassle from Fintan.

Sitting down at his desk, Jason pulled his mobile from his bag, and started playing one of the games on it.

'*Indigo, this is Orange. Commence second phase of testing.*'

Jason ignored the voice, glancing over to see if Fintan might have heard it. The swot was still writing. Probably poetry or something stupid like that.

'*Roger that Orange.*'

There was a tapping at the window, and Jason looked up. There was a kid he didn't recognise leering in at Fintan. He reminded Jason of somebody, but he couldn't think who. He had weird eyes, like the pupils were too big or something, so hardly any of the white showed at all. He had really bushy eyebrows for a kid. His teeth were very crooked too, and his face looked like it was packed with rocks. The boy gazed in at Fintan and gestured with his finger to come out. Fintan turned away, staring down at his book and grinding his teeth. The other boy sneered at him, drawing his nails down the outside of the glass, and then walked away.

'Who's that?' Jason asked.

'You mean you saw him too?' Fintan raised his head.

"Course I saw him, ya eejit. Who was he?'

Fintan regarded him for a moment, to see if this might be leading to a slagging, but Jason looked genuinely interested.

'Nobody else seems to notice him,' Fintan mumbled. 'He's new. I think he might be from the other fifth class, or maybe one of the sixths.'

Their school was a senior primary, it had two of each class from third up to sixth.

'Thought he might be your big brother or something,' Fintan sniffed.

Jason's face twisted into a sneer.

'My *brother*? I don't have a brother! What the hell are you on about?'

'Well, he looks like you … a bit, I mean.'

'I don't look like *that!* That guy looks like a … like a … a flippin' *cave-boy* or somethin' like that.'

Fintan giggled a little, and Jason found himself smirking too.

'Is he giving you hassle?' he asked.

'What do you care?' Fintan retorted.

Jason didn't reply immediately, but he realised that he did care. There was something nasty about that strange kid, and although Jason would never have thought of Fintan as a friend, the swot was in his class, and that counted for something. His posse gave Fintan a hard time, but they were just having a laugh, it wasn't anything serious. He might be a prat, but he was *their* prat.

'Just let me know if he starts messin' with you,' Jason grunted, not wanting to sound too friendly.

Fintan nodded, and there was a cautious, thankful look on his face. It made Jason feel good, seeing that look. He left the swot alone for the rest of the break; there wasn't much fun in picking on him when the other lads weren't there anyway.

* * *

Struggling through Irish class, Jason could not keep his mind off the voices he had heard. He had seen films where people heard voices, and those people were always mad ... or maybe possessed, or living in haunted houses. He was pretty sure that he wasn't mad (at least, not in the unhip, sick-in-the-head way), that was the kind of thing that happened to grown-ups – they'd been around for longer, and had more reason to be loopy. Some of the teachers, for instance, were definitely on their way to being fruit-cakes, and anyone who wanted to spend *the rest of their lives in school* couldn't be right in the head to start with; but you just didn't see many gone-in-the-head loopers his age.

And he wasn't possessed either, as far as he could tell. He hadn't turned grey and wrinkly or started speaking weird, ancient languages (apart from Irish, of course, which he was useless at) and his eyes hadn't started glowing yellow. So it wasn't possession.

That only left haunting. And it was all too easy to believe the school might be haunted. If he was going to haunt anywhere after he died, it would definitely be his school. He figured they had it coming.

'I think the school might be haunted,' he whispered to Vince.

'That's only old Mr Mitchell,' Vince muttered

back. 'He just *looks* dead. No one with a beating heart should be that white.'

Jason stifled a laugh, which Miss Taylor heard, and swivelled to give him a hard stare.

'No, but seriously ...' Jason began again, once the teacher's back was safely again.

But he was interrupted by a tapping on the window. It was that boy again, the one who was hassling Fintan. Fintan was gawping back at him.

'What does he want?' Jason murmured.

'Who?' Vince lifted his head to look in the same direction.

'Him. Your man in the window.'

'Who?'

It was at this moment that Jason knew how this was going to go. He had seen it in enough films. He would insist the kid was standing there, outside the window, and Vince – who obviously couldn't see him – would think Jason was seeing things and ... well, everyone knew what happened then. Jason was having none of that.

'He's gone now,' he lied, still staring at the strange kid's face.

'Jason!' Miss Taylor snapped. 'You won't find the answer to those questions outside in the yard.'

'Yes, Miss,' he mumbled.

But Fintan continued to look, his face frozen in that look he always had when he was about to cry, as the boy in the window smiled eerily, and drew a finger across his throat.

6

More Victims

Fintan went home at lunchtime. Miss Taylor had found him sitting in a corner of the yard, shivering, and decided he was sick. His mother came in and picked him up. Jason wandered around the school, trying to catch sight of the ghost. It *had* to be a ghost; what other answer could there be? His posse wandered with him, but he refused to say what was up. His teeth were tingling again, and he had a real urge to poke at his gums to stop them itching. He couldn't keep his tongue away from the metal, it was like having something stuck between his teeth, except this was stuck to *all* of his teeth.

'Look at what Spit's wearing today,' Vince said,

suddenly. 'Check it out.'

Brian Swift – or Spit as he was known – was in sandals. Only hippies, crusties and saps wore sandals. A serious slagging was in order.

'This one's mine,' Vince announced.

'No way,' Jason held him back. 'This calls for a strategy, this does.'

'... and remember,' Jason said finally. 'Nobody says anything until I ask him where he parks his camel.'

Then they turned, and headed across the yard towards their target. Jason caught his breath when he saw the ghost kid walk from nowhere and start to circle Spit. Spit froze as the boy sauntered around him, hissing something to him, baring his teeth and twisting his face up. So the thing was after Spit too.

'Hey!' Jason barked. 'Hold it!'

His posse stopped, and looked at him expectantly. But Jason strode on, hurrying towards the other two boys.

'I SEE YOU!' he yelled, running at the strange figure, who was ignoring him completely.

Spit turned to find Jason running straight at him, and Jason saw tears in his eyes, and like Fintan, he was grinding his teeth. Spit bolted like a scared rabbit, sprinting into the school. And then the other boy disappeared – turning to wisps of smoke and vanishing.

Jason stumbled to a halt, his heart beating like a machine-gun. He couldn't get his head around it. Part of him never really believed the boy was a ghost, and then to see him just ... just *vanish* like that ...

'Nice one, Jayo,' Vince said from behind him. '"I see you". Nice one. What kind of slaggin' is that? You're losin' your edge, man.'

'Kiss my arse!' Jason snarled at him.

'Orange, this is Indigo. Did you get that?'

Vince was saying something, but all Jason could hear was the crackling voice, louder than ever in his head.

'That's a roger, Indigo. Subject Alpha was definitely reacting to the Tormentor.'

Not in his head. In his mouth. Jason put a hand up to his lips.

'We didn't anticipate this. This may call for more direct action, Indigo,' the voice continued. *'Something may have to be done about that boy.'*

'What's up, Jayo?' Tony asked. 'Your braces at you?'

Jason nodded, but didn't say anything. First the ghost and then this. What was going on? Dr Shapiro had said the braces were experimental, but he hadn't mentioned anything about hearing voices – or seeing weird psycho ghost boys. That oddball orthodontist had some explaining to do. What the hell had he put in Jason's mouth?

Jason shivered. The last words he had heard from his teeth echoed in his head. *Something may have to be done about that boy.*

*   *   *

The rest of the day passed without another sighting of the strange boy, or hearing any of the voices from his teeth. Jason shrugged the strap of his bag onto his shoulder when the bell went, and shuffled towards the door, his mind turning over what he had seen and heard that day. The brief sunny spell they'd had during the week had disappeared, and dark grey clouds brooded overhead as he walked outside. The air had turned cold, and the effect was of a winter's day, gloomy and chill. At the front of the school where the cars and buses pulled up, he saw the Singh Twins standing off to one side on their own. Anita was crying, and Sonia had her arm around her sister's shoulders.

'What's wrong with her?' Jason inquired, walking up to them.

Sonia rounded on him, and he could tell she'd been crying too.

'Why don't you get lost!' she spat, glaring out of red-rimmed eyes. 'We hate the lot of you – you're all as bad as each other!'

He stopped dead in his tracks, and reflexively donned his innocent look – except this time it was for real.

'What are you on about?

'Don't come the innocent with us, Jason McGinty,' Sonia hissed, her face creased in rage. 'You're a worm, your mates are worms, and that brother of yours is the biggest worm of all! Now get lost and leave us alone!'

'What do you mean, my *brother*? I don't have a—'

Jason was going to have a go at her, his temper fired by hers, but he shut his mouth. What could he say? That they were seeing a ghost? That would go down well. Better not to say anything, and avoid getting into those stupid situations they always got into in films. And why did everyone think this thing was his brother? He smothered his anger, and shifted his strap on his shoulder.

'He's not my brother,' he muttered. 'I don't know who he is.'

Turning away, he walked slowly back to the gang of kids waiting to be picked up by their mums. His mobile rang in his bag, and he pulled it out. It was his mother.

'Jason? Listen, I've got held up at work. Could you ask Vince's mum to drop you home? I'll be back in a little while.'

'Yeah, no problem,' he replied.

'Thanks. I'll see you later. Love you! Bye!'

Looking around, he realised Vince was already gone, but Jason felt like a walk anyway. His mum was always trying to get him to walk; it was only a couple of miles. As he started walking, the air grew colder, and he zipped up his jacket, hoping it wasn't going to rain.

The school sat in the middle of a huge bunch of housing estates; there was no straight route back to his house, but Jason knew a short-cut across a foot-ball field and over a wall that would knock fifteen minutes off his journey. The rain started to fall when he was halfway across the park, and the clouds crowded out what was left of the sunlight, plunging him into an early, grey dusk.

There was someone ahead of him, near the edge of the field, and they were coming towards him. As he drew closer, Jason felt a chill down his spine. It was the boy. The ghost. He stopped as Jason came towards him, standing with his hands in his pockets, a sneering smile on his face.

'Who are you?' Jason shouted at him through the rain.

'None of your business,' the boy called back. 'You're not even supposed to know about me. I'm not here for you. Not yet, anyway.'

Jason shivered.

'Are you a ghost?' he asked.

The boy laughed, and quickly crossed the last stretch of ground between them. With a start, Jason noticed that the other boy wasn't wet from the rain. The kid glared wide-eyed at him. His whites were barely visible, the eyes filled with huge, dark discs.

'The Ghost Of The Future,' he chuckled. 'Like in that film? *A Christmas Carol*? Like that. I'm what's comin'. You'll all know me before long.'

His dark hair hung over his forehead in an untidy mop that nearly reached his thick eyebrows.

Something about his lumpy face made Jason hate him; it wasn't just that horrible smile, but the sheer nastiness of it. Like he'd grown up being nasty, and it had twisted his face into this ugly mask.

'I don't know what you're doin' here,' Jason gritted his teeth, feeling them grind together. 'But I'm not scared of you.'

'Yes, you are,' the kid grinned. 'I

can see it in ya. I know everythin' about you. I know you pick your nose, I know you have smelly feet and you hate washing your hair. I know you cry sometimes because you hate your teeth. I know what you eat for dinner. I know where you *live*. You're a dirty, smelly, nose-pickin', chicken-boy cry-baby, and you're all alone out here with me.'

He leaned his face very close to Jason's.

'And I know you're really, *really* frightened of things you don't understand.'

And with that he disappeared, right in front of Jason's eyes. The rain fell through the wisps of smoke he had left behind.

Jason ran. He scrambled over the wall on the other side of the field, and kept running until he stumbled up to the porch of his house, fumbled the key into the lock, and fell in the door. His teeth were fizzing as if they had pins and needles, like you get in your foot when you've been sitting on it for too long watching the telly. Eager to do anything to forget his disturbing encounter, he decided he had

to get these braces sorted; this tingling was going to drive him mad. His mother wasn't home from work, but he couldn't wait.

Picking up the phone, he punched in the number for the orthodontist's.

'Hello?' the receptionist's voice answered.

'Itsch Jayshun McGinchy,' Jason spluttered into the handset. 'Ah nid choo feak choo Jocda Shafiro. Itsch wealy urshent.'

Fortunately, the receptionist was well used to speaking to people whose mouths didn't work properly. Like dentists, orthodontists regularly listened to what their patients had to say while they had their hand stuffed into their patients' mouths.

'Certainly,' the woman replied. 'Just a moment.'

Shapiro's chirpy voice came on the line.

'Hello, Jason! How are the braces? I've been getting some funny readings off them here. You haven't been eating any mobile phones, have you? Ha, ha! Everything all right?'

'No,' Jason replied. 'Jer graces aw jooin' shum funny shtuff. Ah nid joo to sheck jem.'

'Can't have them doing any funny stuff, can we? Let's make an appointment for tomorrow, shall we? Get you all squared away. Would nine fifteen be all right?'

'Datsch purrfick,' Jason grunted.

'That's great, we'll see you then.'

Jason put down the phone, and went looking for some ice cream.

7

No Help At All

Nightmares plagued his sleep that night. He had visions of being wrapped up with wire and his jaws turning inside out and swallowing his own head whole. Dr Shapiro appeared, waving his tiny hands and snipping at the wire with a weensy little pair of pliers. Then Jason was running away from his own teeth, which chased him on metal legs, as they snapped at him. They changed into the ghostly bully, and Jason ran in terror until the only place to go was up the phone mast outside the school. He climbed it, but the bully came after him, and with nowhere else to go, scared out of his mind by the ghost boy, Jason leapt from the top of the

mast and fell
screaming towards
the ground.

He woke up to
find himself
clinging to the
bed. Nervous
and exhausted, he
rolled out of bed
and got ready for
the visit to Dr
Shapiro.

*   *   *

'Well, the computer hasn't been picking up anything unusual,' the orthodontist sighed, gazing into Jason's mouth. 'You're not the first child to think they're picking up radio transmissions on their braces—'

'It's not just radio signals,' Jason exclaimed. 'I'm

seeing things too. And it all started after you put these things in!'

It was then that he realised that this man was the only person who could help. He knew what the braces were capable of, but more importantly, he *didn't* know what *Jason* was capable of. There was no way his mother or teachers would take him seriously if he told them what he thought was going on; they had all heard too many lies from his mis-shapen mouth. So now, with no one else he could trust, he told his orthodontist what had been happening at school. Shapiro listened quietly, with a raised eyebrow.

'Yes, well. Maybe all this tingling is triggering your imagination. Let's hook you up with a direct connection and see if there's anything we've missed. Open wide!'

Shapiro took what looked like a large, flat baby's soother and put it in Jason's gaping mouth. It had wires running from the handle end, which connected with the laptop on the counter.

'Bite down, that's a good boy.'

Jason caught a glimpse of himself in the polished surface of a steel cupboard door. With this thing in his mouth, he looked like a big baby in a car-seat. He  prayed that nobody would come in and see him like this. At least there were blinds covering the windows.

'Now, we'll just download the data,' Shapiro was saying to himself, tapping away at the keyboard.

The screen suddenly went a blank grey.

'What's this now—?' he punched a few more of the keys.

At first, nothing happened. Then part of the screen went lighter, and an image started to appear. It was a creepy face, with bushy eyebrows, unruly black hair, and dark, piercing eyes.

'Crikey! What the blazes is that?'

Sparks burst from the laptop, and then there was a crackling sound, and all the lights went out.

Dr Shapiro was standing in the dark with his tiny hands covering his face. Reaching over with one hand, he opened the blinds on the window. He peered through the fingers of his other hand at Jason.

'Are you all right?' he whispered. 'What on earth just happened? What was that thing?'

Jason spat out the big soother and glared at his orthodontist.

'That's what I've been trying to tell you about! Are you going to listen to me now, or what?'

'I'm sorry, Jason, but I don't see what I can do,' Shapiro avoided his gaze. 'You should go and tell your mother. She'll take your story to the police, I'm sure. They'll help you.'

'You're the only one who can help,' Jason insisted, in desperation. 'Nobody else will believe me; I've got a bit of a reputation ... Anyway, that doesn't matter. You saw the ghost bully thing, and you know what these braces can do. You've got to help.'

The orthodontist was fiddling with his burnt-out laptop. Jason frantically tried to come up with some way of spurring the man into action.

'Dr Shapiro, this thing ... this ghost? It's making the kids *grind their teeth*!'

For a few seconds, Shapiro's face was set in a look of absolute shock. Clearly, the idea of something causing such damage to children's teeth filled him with horror. Jason thought he was finally getting through. But it was no use; the orthodontist turned away and picked up a pen.

'How about if I write a note about this to your mother?' he offered, without looking around. 'How about that?'

Shapiro was a grown-up, and grown-ups thought everything could be solved by going to some authority or other. And what good would teachers or the police do against a spectre that could appear and disappear whenever it liked? Jason pulled the napkin from under his chin, threw it in the bin, and walked out. He would just have to deal with this thing on his own.

8

Drawing Monsters

Jason showed up late for school. He didn't go in immediately. He stood behind one of the legs of the huge phone mast that towered over the empty lot across the road from the school. The bell was going and all the kids in the yard were lining up to go in. Fintan was back, and Jason waited to see if the ghost boy would be there to pick on him again. But there was no sign of the spectre. With no idea what to do next, Jason hurried across the road to the now-empty yard.

A horn blared at him, making him jump, and he bounded backwards just in time to avoid being hit by a large, white van with darkened windows. It

swept past, and down the road. There was a sign on the side, saying:

Spectron Educational Supplies: Helping Build Better Children.

'Road hog!' Jason roared after it.

It pulled in to the kerb and stopped. Deciding he should make himself scarce, Jason trotted into the schoolyard. He realised his teeth were tingling again, worse than ever.

'*Orange, this is Mauve. We are in position. Ready to begin next testing phase.*'

Jason stopped in mid-stride, listening intently to the voices coming from his teeth.

'*That's a roger, Mauve. Is Subject Alpha clear of the testing area?*'

'*Affirmative, Orange. The boy is out in the yard – we nearly ran over the little idiot. We're looking at him now, over.*'

Jason swivelled slowly to stare at the van. He could see nothing through the dark windows. Swallowing a lump in his throat, he considered going over. No, he thought. No way. He ran on into the school, and hurried to his class.

They were doing art, and Miss Taylor had already given out paper and colouring pencils.

'All right,' she was saying. 'Seeing as everybody seems to be in such a dark mood, I want you all to come up with a monster. Go mad with it – I want to see some really nasty beasts!'

Tony was sitting in Jason's usual seat beside Vince, so the only free chair was beside Fintan. Heaving a disgusted sigh, Jason sat down and took out his pencil case. Miss Taylor gave him a sheet of paper, and he began to create a creature that looked like a carnivorous truck. Out of the corner of his eye, he noticed Fintan's monster was quite different. It was a boy with dark hair, solid black eyes, and bad teeth.

'Very creepy, Fintan,' Miss Taylor said from behind them. 'But who's copying who, here?'

Jason looked up at her, and back at Fintan's drawing. Then he glanced past Fintan at what the Singh Twins were doing. They too, had drawn the dead-eyed ghost boy. From various points around him, he could hear the quiet grinding of teeth. Without thinking, Jason stood up, and walked around the class.

'Jason!' the teacher barked. 'Get back to your seat!'

He didn't hear her. He was looking at the pictures. They were all different styles, but they all showed the same thing. The boy with the black hair, the dark eyes, the jagged teeth, and the pale, lumpy face. Every kid in the class was drawing the ghost. They'd all seen him.

'Jason! Miss Taylor's voice snapped him out of his reverie.

'Sorry, Miss.'

'Sit down. And the rest of you, try and be a little more original ...' she paused, looking down at the drawings around her, and then over at Jason. 'My

God, Jason. I never even realised. I'm sorry.'

Before he could ask her what she meant, she slammed the book she was holding down on her desk, making them all jump.

'I don't know what you're all playing at, but it's a horrible thing to do,' she shouted. 'I want you all to tear those pictures up, and apologise to Jason right now!'

Most of them looked genuinely surprised that others had drawn the same thing. Some of the children started tearing up their pages. But Tony held onto his, looking away, and Vince folded his arms defiantly, casting a sullen eye at Jason.

'I'm not apologising for nothin'', he said.

'Then you can go and see the principal,' Miss Taylor retorted.

Jason was no longer listening. From all around him, he could feel the hateful stares of his classmates. They had all seen the mysterious bully; they all had that scared, furtive look in their eyes. This thing was coming after all of them now.

'What are you all looking at me for?' he blurted out. 'It's not me! You know it's not!'

In a moment of shock, he realised he was crying. He was blubbering like a little kid in front of his class.

'Go to hell, the lot o' yiz!' he shrieked, and ran out of the classroom.

Miss Taylor was calling out from behind him, but he kept on running. Out of the school, across the yard, and out the gate. He charged straight across the road without even looking for oncoming cars, and slammed into the side of the white van, hammering on the door.

'Get out, get out, get out, GET OUT OF THERE YOU RATS!'

Jason felt a sharp tingle in his teeth again, and instinctively went to scratch the imaginary itch with his fingernail. But the tingling in his braces rose like a fizzy drink exploding in his mouth, his head suddenly filled with white noise, deafening him.

'Aaaugh!' he screamed, falling to the ground.

He covered his ears, but it didn't make any difference. The side-door to the back of the van slid open, and two men stepped out.

'He could pick up the signal, then,' Jason heard one of them say over the noise in his skull.

'We'll just have to see that never happens again, won't we?' the other one said.

That was all Jason heard, because at that point – much to his relief – he fainted.

9

A Secret Government
Plot

The voices seemed very far away at first.

'It must be his braces,' someone said, in a gravelly growl. 'They're acting as a receiver. Picking up all our transmissions. They're weird. Never seen anything like them before.'

'Can we pull them off?' another, watery voice asked.

'Not without pulling out his teeth too. I'm no orthodontist.'

'It's just braces; it can't be that hard!' the watery one insisted.

'Look at his teeth, for goodness sake!' the gravelly

voice whined. 'It's like some kind of tooth bomb went off in his mouth. And there's enough wire in there to hook up some Christmas tree lights. I can't do it, I'm tellin' you. Not without taking out the teeth.'

Jason was wide awake now, but he stayed perfectly still, despite being terrified.

'With teeth like that, we'd be doing the little brat a favour—' the weaker voice paused. 'Hey! You awake?'

A hand slapped Jason's face.

'Stop faking, you little maggot. Look at me!'

Jason opened his eyes.

He was in some kind of computer lab. Banks of technical-looking machines with screens and lights on them lined the walls. There was a hum of a hundred little fans running, and the smell of warm metal and dust was in the air. He was strapped to a stainless steel table shaped like a big fat 'X'. A mass of cameras and needles and other gadgets hung from an arm above his head that reminded him of the lamp in the orthodontist's.

There were three men in the room, all wearing long, dark coats and black sunglasses, even though it was warm, and there weren't even any windows to let the sun in. Jason hated people who wore sunglasses indoors. The two really big guys looked almost exactly alike, except one was black, and one was white. They both had tight haircuts and designer stubble. The other man was smaller and chubbier, with fuzzy red hair, half-closed eyes, and an untidy goatee beard.

'Let me go!' Jason shouted, pulling at the straps.

'Whoa, we've got a wild one here!' the goateed one said, the one with the watery voice. 'Calm down, kid. Don't have a conniption! Steady now, we're not going to hurt you, are we boys?'

'No way,' the big white guy said. He had the gravelly voice.

'We're not out to hurt anyone,' the big black guy added. He had a gravelly voice too. Almost exactly the same as his mate. Jason wondered if that ever got confusing.

'These are just to stop you hurting yourself,' the watery-voiced one waved at the straps holding Jason's wrists and ankles. 'And so you don't go damaging our equipment. Nothing personal. You can call me Agent Orange, by the way. And these are Agents Indigo and Mauve.'

The two big guys nodded. Jason wondered which was which.

'What's going on?' he asked in a surly tone.

'I'm afraid you've stumbled upon a secret government plot,' Agent Orange gave him an exaggerated frown. 'A highly classified educational project. Even your teachers don't know about it. In fact, you're an important part of this project – even a vital one, you might say.'

'Yeah, vital,' one of the henchmen grunted with a smile.

Jason said nothing. He knew that this was where the bad guys would tell him everything, and he had to concentrate on escaping, so that he could get this out in the open and defeat the plot. That was how John Crater always did it in the *Fireflight* films. Bad guys couldn't help themselves, they had to boast about how smart they were. That was always their undoing.

'But anyway, enough of that,' Orange stood up and went over to a control panel, and touched the commands on one of the screens. 'We can't go telling you all our plans, can we? Give me a minute here, and we'll just pull those braces off – hopefully we'll leave most of your teeth where they are – and then I'll erase your memory ... just the last couple of days or so, and then we'll send you back to school. Lie back and relax, this won't take long.'

Jason gazed up in horror at the apparatus hanging

over him. Orange leaned in to attach a chain to his braces with a set of small claws. The other end of the chain was wrapped round a winch hanging from the ceiling.

'I would say that this won't hurt,' he said, making a friendly grimace. 'But it probably will.'

'Wait!' Jason exclaimed, his eyes as wide as saucers at the sight of the claws. He knew exactly how solidly those braces were bound to his teeth. 'Aren't you ... I mean ...' His mind raced, as he tried to think of some way of keeping those claws away from his mouth. He couldn't come up with anything – and so he did what came naturally. 'To hell with it – *pull* out my braces then! You think I'm scared of you? *Wipe* my memory, you pigs. I don't want to remember you anyway. Who would? I mean look at you, tryin' to look cool; wearin' sunglasses inside and dressing like a bunch of ... of science fiction nerds. When's the UFO due? Secret agents? You must be kiddin'! You look more like a sad pack o' mummy's boys tryin' to be with it. And what's with your *names*? I mean, *colours*? That's like from a *kid's* programme isn't it? What are you, cartoon characters? Or are you just a gang of big girls' blouses?' He put on a girlie voice. 'Oh I want to be *Agent Indigo* – it, like, y'know, so goes with my *handbag...*'

Orange was looking back at Mauve and Indigo, grinning.

'This is good stuff. We should be recording this.'

'... Oh, I want to be *Agent Mauve,*' Jason went on.

'That way I can, like, paint my *nails* with my *name*, won't that be so cool?'

He ran out of breath, and let out a burst of gasping laughter that surprised him as much as them. There was a sweet smell in the air that reminded Jason of something that he couldn't put his finger on. Agent Orange was giggling as he reached over and pressed a button on the control panel. Then he continued attaching the cable to Jason's braces.

'No, no,' he waved at Jason, chuckling. 'Keep going, we can use this.'

'Whah aw yow kalkin' abou'?' Jason demanded, around Agent Orange's fingers. He was feeling dizzy now, and for reasons he couldn't understand, the idea of having all his teeth pulled out in one go was starting to seem quite funny.

'We came to your school trying to find all the meanest, slimiest, nastiest, most horrible bullies in the area for our experiments,' Orange told him with a big grin, as he took out a small screwdriver and started adjusting the claws gripping Jason's braces.

'All the imaginative little rat pieces of lowlife scum. And you were one of our stars!'

Jason sniggered, but the man's words hurt more than he wanted to admit. He wasn't a real bully. It wasn't like he was evil or anything; he was just having a laugh. Jason McGinty wasn't the bad guy. He was like John Crater – a good guy with some rough edges. So what if he slagged people off sometimes? He tried pulling at the straps again, but he was held tight. Orange went on making tiny adjustments here and there to the cluster of claws. Jason's heart was beating like a drum in a dance tune, and he was covered in sweat, but he still found himself giggling.

10

Laughing In The Face Of Fear

'You see, life changes after your school years, Jason,' Agent Orange went on, grinning. '*You* rule in the yard, and whenever the teacher's not around. But later on? Those swots you're bullying are going to become scientists and politicians and businessmen. Heh, heh, heh. They're going to be *your bosses*. While you're busy having a good time, and worrying about being popular, they're paying attention. Heh, heh. They're learning how to get ahead. They're picking up *skills*.

'But a bunch of the nerds in power now want to get rid of bullying in schools forever. So we were brought in study bullies and their victims ... to see how their minds worked. I invented a low frequency wave that can beam a bully right into your brain! We used thugs like you to create the perfect bully, the *Tormentor*, and we've been testing it on kids all over the area. We can read their hidden thoughts – that's the secret, you see. Everybody's got a weakness, and you can use it to make their lives a misery.'

Orange's face was contorted into an insane grin as he made the last few delicate tweaks.

'The only thing was, we got to *like* it. Heh, heh, heh. Ha, ha. It was supposed to be just research – but damn it, Jason, it's just so much fun! The Tormentor can drive a child mad with despair.'

With a flourish, he touched a command on a screen. The ghost bully, the Tormentor, appeared at the foot of the X-shaped table. And now Jason understood why all the kids had started turning on him. It *did* look like him, but its teeth weren't as bad, and its face was uglier, lumpier. It could have been a nastier, Neanderthal version of him. And suddenly, he wasn't laughing any more. Just looking at it made him grind his teeth with rage and frustration. He didn't want to be like that thing. He didn't want to be hated.

'I'm not like that,' he growled. 'I'm not like you.'

Agent Orange brought his face close to Jason's, giggling uncontrollably.

'Oh but … ha, ha … but you are, Jason. Ha, ha, ha! We're exactly alike.' He paused, and then whispered. 'I get a thrill, every time I make one of them cry.'

His fingers probed into Jason's mouth, checking that the claws were properly fixed.

'The Tormentor's only supposed to be seen by the kids we target, but you've been picking up the signals on your braces, so they've got to come off.'

His fingers tickled, and Jason found himself starting to laugh again.

'Whuh ... Ha, ha ha,' Orange sniffled. 'Whuh ... What's so funny? Ha, ha, ha, ha. Shut your eyes now, and we'll have those teeth ... I mean those braces out in no time.'

Jason burst into hysterical laughter around Orange's fingers – and then his jaws slammed shut. The agent screamed, trying to tug his trapped fingers free of Jason's ferocious teeth. Indigo and Mauve watched

him struggling with both his hands caught in the boy's mouth, and exploded into shrieks of laughter.

Jason tried to help, but found he couldn't open his jaws. They were no longer under his control. He laughed so hard drool spat from the sides of his mouth. Orange was cackling and crying out in frustration at the same time. Indigo and Mauve were rolling around on the floor, with tears rolling down their faces. The more Orange struggled, the harder they laughed.

And then the door on the other side of the room swung open, and Jason saw a familiar figure standing there. Dr Shapiro put down the gas cylinder he was holding. He was wearing a gas mask, and he walked quickly over to the two agents on the floor. Forcing their jaws open, he jammed something metal into each of their mouths. Straightening up, he strode over to the table where Jason was biting down on Orange's fingers. The orthodontist pinched the agent's nose, forcing him to open his mouth, and slipped something inside. Jason heard a clicking sound, and when Shapiro withdrew his hand, he saw that Orange now wore a crude, bulky set of braces.

'Snap-on braces,' the orthodontist told them. 'Still experimental, but useful nonetheless.'

Ignoring the projection of the Tormentor – which he couldn't see – he took out a small remote control and pressed a button. Jason's jaws unlocked, and Agent Orange pulled his fingers free. He stuck them under his armpits and danced around in pain. Jason laughed deliriously.

'Whuh's goin' on?' he managed to gasp.

'Easy there, Jason,' Shapiro said. 'It's just laughing gas. I fed it through the door to disable our friends here. You'll calm down in a few minutes. When your braces registered that they were in danger, they signalled me and I came running. It's lucky I came prepared.'

He carefully detached the claws and chain and then checked Jason's mouth. Then he undid the straps.

'You'll be right as rain,' he assured him.

Indigo and Mauve were getting serious now. They got to their feet, rubbing their cheeks, which must have been aching from the laughing.

'You'll pay for that,' Indigo hissed.

They started forward, fists raised. Shapiro touched another button on his control, and suddenly, the two thugs' faces slammed together, their mouths jammed up against each other, as if these two muscle-bound agents were enjoying a passionate snog.

'I've just magnetised your braces,' Shapiro told them. 'Behave, or I'll set them to biting mode.'

Orange was pulling at the braces in his mouth. Shapiro gave him a nasty look.

'And as for you ...' he said in a venomous voice. 'You have some explaining to do. And you're going to tell me everything, or I'll switch your braces to mangle mode, and you'll end up with teeth like his.'

He pointed at Jason, who gave Agent Orange a big, wide smile. Orange stared at those misshapen

molars and shrieked, frantically trying to pull the braces from his teeth. But it was no use, they were stuck fast.

'You go on home, Jason,' Shapiro said, pointing towards the door. 'I'll handle this now. We're not far from the school, just turn right on the road and keep going. These gentlemen and I are going to have a little chat.'

Jason wanted to stay and watch that little chat, but Shapiro's tone left no room for argument. He slipped down off the table, and scurried towards the door.

Behind him, he could hear Shapiro saying, as he opened the leather bag he had with him:

'This all comes to an end now, gentlemen. If you mess with a child's teeth, you mess with the entire dental profession.'

Jason ran along the dark, dingy corridor, out an emergency door, and across a deserted car park. He kept running until he got home.

* * *

Jason never saw Agent Orange, or his henchmen, or their van again. The Tormentor was gone, but the other kids in school still gave Jason strange looks from time to time. Mostly though, things got back to normal, and he even got used to having those mad braces on his teeth.

He didn't see much of Dr Shapiro, and when he did, the orthodontist wouldn't tell him what he had done to the secret agents. All he said was that Jason and his friends didn't have to worry any more. From the way he said it, Jason believed him.

And as for being a bully? Well, you couldn't quite say he was cured. He still gave a slagging and took the mickey, and he was still a bit of smart-arse. But he wasn't so nasty about it any more, and he didn't mind if the others slagged him back.

Unless somebody made a crack about his teeth, of course. He'd still lay into them for that. But then, nobody's perfect.